For Doctor John and his animals

First American edition published in 1991 by Philomel Books,
a division of The Putnam & Grosset Book Group,
200 Madison Avenue, New York, NY 10016.
Originally published in Japanese in 1990 by Kaisei-Sha Publishing Co., Ltd.,
Tokyo, under the title *Doctor John No Doubutsuen*.
English translation rights arranged with Kaisei-Sha Publishing Co., Ltd.,
through Japan Foreign-Rights Centre.
Published simultaneously in Canada.
Printed in Hong Kong by South China Printing Co. (1988) Ltd.

Library of Congress Cataloging-in-Publication Data
Ichikawa, Satomi. [Dr. John no doubutsuen. English] Nora's duck/by
Satomi Ichikawa. p. cm. Translation of: Dr. John no doubutsuen.
Summary: Nora finds a duckling in the woods and takes it to Doctor
John, who provides love and care for many wild and domestic animals
who have come to grief.
ISBN 0-399-21805-X
[1. Ducks—Fiction. 2. Animals—Fiction. 3. Wildlife rescue—Fiction.]
I. Title. PZ7.I16Nq 1991 90-20160 CIP AC [E]—dc20

First impression

Nora's Duck
Satomi Ichikawa

Philomel Books   New York

One warm spring day, Nora and her three friends—
Maggie the doll, Teddy the stuffed bear, and Kiki the
dog—went into the woods.

Suddenly, Kiki, who had been running on ahead by
himself, stopped in front of a thicket and began barking.
When Nora peeped into the thicket, she saw a little
brown ball of fluff.

It was a baby duckling, with its eyes closed. Nora put
the duckling into her hat.

"It's ill. Let's take it to Doctor John," said Teddy the bear.

"Doctor John isn't an animal doctor…" said Maggie, looking
worried.

"That doesn't matter now," Nora said. "We must hurry."

When he heard Nora say this, Kiki dashed off across the field in
the direction of Doctor John's house.

Doctor John examined the duckling carefully. Then he said to Nora, "It doesn't seem to have any serious injuries. It was probably attacked by another animal while it was playing on the pond in the woods. There's no need to worry."

"We'll put it into the bird hospital and let it rest."
"Bird hospital?" said Nora. Maggie looked surprised.
Doctor John nodded and took the duckling into the shed.

"This is where I keep the birds who are ill or injured or too old to walk. We'll leave the duckling here for a little while."

Doctor John put the duckling into a box. There were birds everywhere.

"What's wrong with this bird?" asked Nora, pointing to a squeaky little bird sitting in a nest.

"That poor thing fell out of its nest. I'm looking after it until it can fly. The duckling will get better too. Wait and see."

"Now I'm going to feed the animals. Will you come with me?"
Doctor John set off in the direction of his garden pond.

"Look, Doctor John. Geese and ducks! Mallards!
Are they all sick?" asked Nora.

"Some were attacked by other animals and some were caught in
traps. A few were hit by cars. Now they've all recovered. But they
still cannot run or fly well, so it would be dangerous for them to
leave." Dr. John might not be an animal doctor, but he surely was
the animals' friend.

In the back garden, near the clothesline, were some hens.
"These hens seem just fine to me," said Nora, looking puzzled.
"They were abandoned by their owners," Doctor John said.
"If animals who have been kept are suddenly thrown out,
they can't live on their own." A cocky red rooster certainly
seemed happy to be there.

Nora saw some sheep busy eating grass in the next field.
They looked like giants to Maggie.

"Why do they leave so many beautiful flowers?" Nora wondered
out loud. "If it was me, I'd eat those flowers first."

"The sheep know that some flowers are poisonous. Some don't
taste good. They can tell which ones. Pretty clever, don't you
think?" Doctor John sounded full of admiration for his sheep.

"This is Rudolf. The one over there is Albert," Doctor John said at the edge of the woods. "Goats don't have thick woolly coats like sheep, so on cold or rainy days they need somewhere to take shelter."

"Why is Rudolf here?" asked Nora. It seemed as if almost everyone had a reason to be there.

"Rudolf was born aboard ship. On long voyages some ships take goats along for fresh milk. But since Rudolf turned out to be a billy goat, they were going to sell him. Instead, they gave him to me. If Rudolf could talk, I'd love to hear him tell what he saw during that voyage."

"So would we!" shouted Nora and her three friends.

At the bottom of a gooseberry bush, Nora found a wooden house. It belonged to a tortoise.

"This tortoise used to live in a warm climate, so he doesn't like the cold," Doctor John explained. "That's why I made him this house. In the winter he moves into my attic. For a long time he belonged to a woman I knew; then he came to me. That was twenty years ago. He must be nearly a hundred tortoise years old now." Doctor John grinned.

When Nora held out some buttercup flowers and wild strawberries, the tortoise poked out his head and hungrily snapped them up.

"This is Polly the parrot," said Doctor John. "My mother used to keep her before I was born."

"Oh, but she's so small! Is she really that old?"

Polly squawked happily and jumped onto Doctor John's arm.

"Polly loves young children like you."

Nora learned that Polly's favorite foods were sunflower seeds, bananas, grapes, and biscuits. She was very pleased when Polly ate a biscuit from her hand. Kiki and Teddy just watched.

Nora and her friends were still meeting new animals when the sun began to go down. In the apple orchard, now bathed in the golden rays of the sun, a donkey was quietly eating grass.

"Hello, Mister Donkey," said Nora. "Do you like carrots?"

The donkey raised its gentle eyes and began to walk toward her.

"Why are the animals living here all so gentle?" asked Nora.

"Perhaps it's because they can all live here free from worry," replied Doctor John. "They know they are being cared for."

"Doctor John, are you an animal doctor?" asked Maggie the doll.
Doctor John laughed. "No, no, I was a doctor for people. But
ever since I stopped doing that job, it seems my animal
patients have increased. Now wouldn't you all like to know what
has happened to the little duckling?"

Doctor John went into his bird hospital and brought out the duckling's box.

"It's better! It can stand up all by itself."
Nora could hardly believe it.

The duckling sat happily on Nora's knee and then on
her shoulder.

"I found this duckling," Nora proudly told the other
animals.

Then, before Nora knew it, the duckling had jumped down from her shoulder and begun walking among the animals. It seemed to be trying to ask them something.

After going around to each animal, the duckling
jumped into Nora's hat, and squeaked over and over again.
"I wish I could understand duck language," Nora
sighed. "What are you trying to say, little duck?"

When it was time for her to go home, Nora still didn't know.

"Doctor John, animals can't speak to us in words. How can we understand what they want?"

"By watching an animal very carefully, you come to know," explained Doctor John.

Maggie looked very carefully at the animals who were looking at her.

"My dear little duckling, what are you trying to say to me?" Nora asked on the way home. She held the duckling in the warmth of her hand, then put it in her hat again and watched it carefully. But she still wasn't sure.

Nora stopped for a moment by the pond in the woods; then she bent down and let the duckling go. How pleased she was when it found its mother and swam happily off behind her!

"How did you know what the duckling was saying to you?" asked Maggie, Teddy, and Kiki, looking at Nora in wonder.

Nora just smiled as she watched the duckling swim away. Then she hurried home across the field to her own mother.

Afterword

For several years now I have spent one or two months of each year with Doctor John and his wife at their home in a small village in Kent, England. Their ivy-covered house, part of which was built originally in the sixteenth century, welcomes me. There is a mysterious quality to it—something old and timeworn, yet serene.

The overgrown trees and flowers of the garden have a rather agreeable feeling of neglect, as if Father Time had been left to tend them. More than anything else, I love to take a chair into a corner of the garden and sketch. At my feet, a duck with an injured leg and a mallard that has lost half of its down waddle around. There is also a goose whose feathers hang loosely. In the meadow beyond, against a green pastoral background, I watch sheep of varying types and sizes grazing in the grass.

The sight of Doctor John emerging from his house carrying a bucket of feed puts the animals into a festive mood. Running or hobbling, they all follow him, each crying out for his attention. The animals in Doctor John's care are all here for a reason: one was attacked by a fox, another was in a traffic accident, others were abandoned because they were ill or old, and so on. Animals who have come to grief can live here peacefully, surrounded by an atmosphere of constant love and care.

Doctor John peeps into my sketchbook. "Drawing? That's the spirit!" he says, patting my head. He comes next to a sheep, "Not eating poisonous plants? That's the spirit!" he says, patting the sheep on the head. Whether they be human or animal, to Doctor John all living things are dear, each worthy of equal respect.

I hope that the small episode I have put into pictures allows you too to enter the world of Doctor John and his animals.

Satomi Ichikawa
April 1990, Paris